Pup 681

A SEA OTTER RESCUE STORY

Jean Reidy   *illustrated by* **Ashley Crowley**

GODWINBOOKS

Henry Holt and Company
New York

Henry Holt and Company, *Publishers since 1866*
Henry Holt® is a registered trademark of Macmillan Publishing Group, LLC
175 Fifth Avenue, New York, NY 10010
mackids.com

Text copyright © 2019 by Jean Reidy
Illustrations copyright © 2019 by Ashley Crowley
All rights reserved.

Library of Congress Control Number: 2018949575
ISBN 978-1-250-11450-1

Our books may be purchased in bulk for promotional, educational, or business use.
Please contact your local bookseller or the Macmillan Corporate and Premium Sales Department at
(800) 221-7945 ext. 5442 or by e-mail at MacmillanSpecialMarkets@macmillan.com.

First edition, 2019 / Designed by Patrick Collins
Printed in China by Hung Hing Off-set Printing Co. Ltd., Heshan City, Guangdong Province

The artist used colored inks applied using a water brush pen, graphite sticks, pastels,
colored pencils, and Adobe Photoshop to create the illustrations for this book.

1 3 5 7 9 10 8 6 4 2

To Sam, with enough love to fill an ocean.
—J. R.

For my beautiful wife, Nicole,
and my darling boy, Frankie X.
—A. C.

*W*hen the moon slipped under the mist
and the sun began to burn through,
a tiny one opened her eyes.

She lay wrapped
snugly in sea kelp
on the sandy shore.

Her stomach stirred,

and her shoulders shivered.

Not even the sun could chase away her chill.

Her cry rose above the roar of the surf.

Would the sun leave her, too?

A huge empty space grew
in her tiny, tiny heart.
A space that, maybe,
once held something—
or someone.

"It's a pup!"

Friendly eyes twinkled from under a cap.
Large, gentle hands lifted her tenderly
and bundled her up tight.

"Hello there, little one!
You're Pup 681!"

Pup 681?
Who?
Me?
she wondered.

She wondered while she traveled far...

. . . to a place with purple kelp
and clear salt pools
and tall, tall glass that looked out
on endless water.

There,
she was warmed

And there,
she discovered
that she was
not a fish

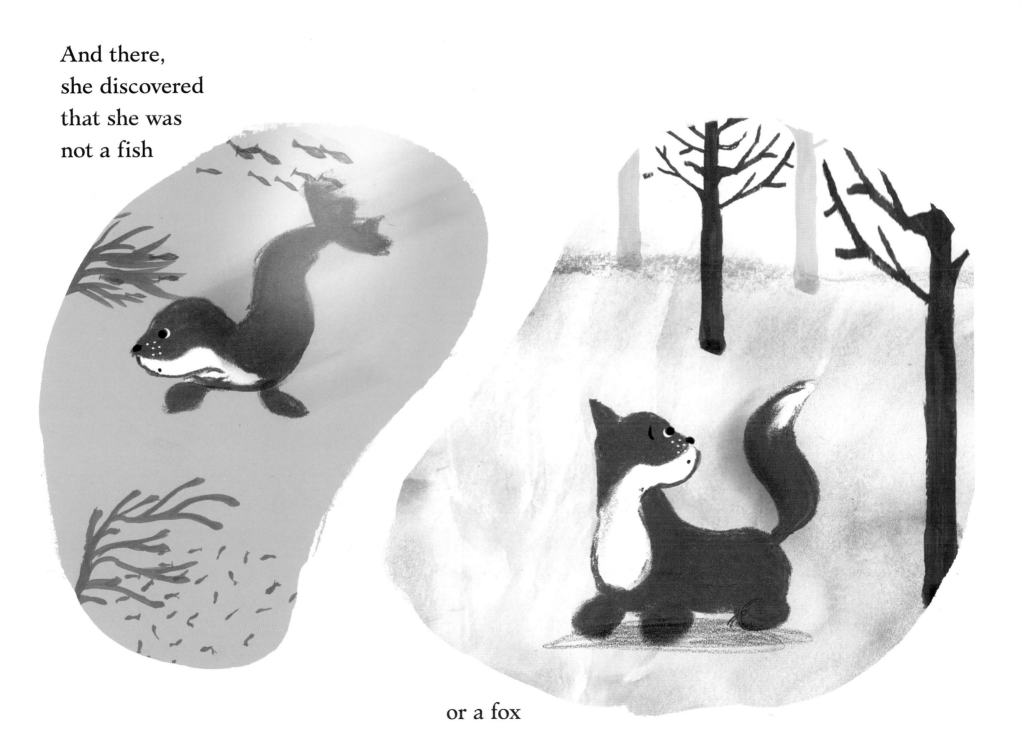

or a fox

and fluffed

and
fed.

or a falcon

but an otter.

Sea Otter Pup 681.

Six hundred eighty-one
was a very big number
for a very small otter.

The pup knew
she must have family
out there in that endless water.

So she tucked a treasure
safely away
in her pocket,
for the day she found them.

As weeks passed, the
playful pup kept busy.

Dive and glide!

Slip and slide!

Seek and hide!

Towel dried!

Very busy!

So busy that sometimes—
right in the middle of it all—
she dozed, and she dreamed
of her family dreaming of her.

Pup 681 . . .
That big, big number
reminded her
of that big, empty space
in her tiny otter heart.

One day,
when the sky turned gray
and the endless waters blackened,
the mist returned.

So did the stirring
and the shivering.

The pup felt like she was back
on the lonely sand beach.
And no blanket of purple kelp
could make it right.

The pup was wrapped—
"Hang on."
And warmed—
"Hang on there."
And fed—
"Hang on, little pup."
Night and day,
and day and night.

It seemed that both the sun and the
moon had left her once and for all.

Until suddenly,
she began to feel the rhythm
of the surf rocking her,
so, so gently, rocking her.

"Hey there!"

And the mist began to lift.

"Hey there, little pup."

And she gazed into tired,
twinkling eyes
in the shadow of a cap—

"That's it."

And she soaked in a smile,
like sunshine breaking through.

"That's it, little friend."

That's it! she thought.

And warmth filled her full,
so very full,
even filling the empty space in her heart.

And she perked.
And she poked.
And she pulled out a treasure.

And she dropped it into those huge,
gentle hands!

Because sometimes family is hundreds,

and sometimes
it is one—
someone—
with enough love to fill an ocean
and who loves YOU

to the moon and back.

DEAR READER,

Pup 681 is a work of fiction. But it is based on the true story of an orphaned sea otter, one of the smallest ever rescued by the Monterey Bay Aquarium. Less than a week old and weighing only two pounds, the pup was found on the California coast and identified as "681"—the 681st otter to enter their otter program. When she was five weeks old, she was moved to her permanent home at the Shedd Aquarium in Chicago.

While in my story I've focused on a single caregiver, Pup 681 in fact received round-the-clock care from several animal care experts. And while it's unlikely that she ever got sick, as portrayed in my story, sea otter pups do have trouble regulating their body temperatures, and the process of sea otter rescue and rehabilitation is fragile and fraught with risk.

Pup 681 won the hearts of millions when her story was picked up and her videos were shared by major news networks. But she became a true celebrity when the Shedd Aquarium teamed up with *Good Morning America* to hold a contest for her naming. She was lovingly renamed Luna . . . a reminder of her original home near Half Moon Bay.

There are loads of adorable Luna videos online. Simply search "pup 681" or check out the Shedd Aquarium website at sheddaquarium.org.

I've fallen in love with Luna, and I hope you do, too!

—JEAN REIDY

FUN SEA OTTER FACTS

- Sea otters have a pocket of loose skin under their forelegs where they store toys, food, and their favorite rocks, which they use as tools.

- Sea otters at Shedd love to wrap themselves in colorful fabric car-wash strips—which resemble sea kelp.

- And the cutest fact EVER: Sea otters often hold hands to make a "raft"—sometimes with hundreds or thousands of other otters—while they sleep, so that they don't drift out to sea.